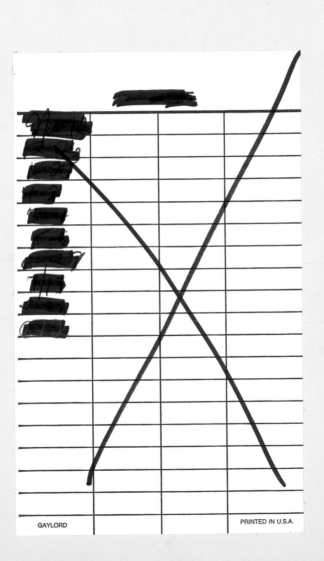

GAYLORD   PRINTED IN U.S.A.

1914

MEET

~~Middletown, RI 02842~~

Rebecca

An American Girl

BY JACQUELINE DEMBAR GREENE

ILLUSTRATIONS ROBERT HUNT

VIGNETTES SUSAN MCALILEY

★AmericanGirl®

9/29/09

THE AMERICAN GIRLS

1764

KAYA, an adventurous Nez Perce girl whose deep love for horses and respect for nature nourish her spirit

1774

FELICITY, a spunky, spritely colonial girl, full of energy and independence

1824

JOSEFINA, a Hispanic girl whose heart and hopes are as big as the New Mexico sky

1854

KIRSTEN, a pioneer girl of strength and spirit who settles on the frontier

1864

ADDY, a courageous girl determined to be free in the midst of the Civil War

1904  SAMANTHA, a bright Victorian beauty, an orphan raised by her wealthy grandmother

1914  REBECCA, a lively girl with dramatic flair growing up in New York City

1934  KIT, a clever, resourceful girl facing the Great Depression with spirit and determination

1944  MOLLY, who schemes and dreams on the home front during World War Two

1974 JULIE, a fun-loving girl from San Francisco who faces big changes—and creates a few of her own

PICTURE CREDITS
The following individuals and organizations have generously
given permission to reprint images contained in "Looking Back":
pp. 72–73—Albert and Temmy Latner Jewish Public Library of Toronto (Hester Street);
The Jewish Museum of New York/Art Resource, NY (shoe shop); © reproduced by permission
of The State Hermitage Museum, St. Petersburg, Russia/Corbis (Tsar); from the archives of
the YIVO Institute for Jewish Research (pogrom); pp. 74–75—courtesy of the Statue of Liberty
National Monument (poster); courtesy Jennifer Hirsch (Russian linens and candlesticks); from
the archives of the YIVO Institute for Jewish Research (King Lear); © Hulton-Deutsch Collection/
Corbis (Marx Brothers); photograph by Whitney Cox © Disney 1997 (theater); pp. 76–77—
© John Springer Collection/Corbis (Pearl White); charity box, ca. 1920. Courtesy of
The Museum of Jewish Heritage, New York. Gift of Dr. David Pollock
and Judy Kirpich (1999.A.572)

Cataloging-in-Publication Data available from the Library of Congress

TO MY MOTHER,
RACHEL B. DEMBAR,
WHO OPENED MY WORLD TO
DOLLS AND BOOKS

Rebecca's parents and grandparents came to America before
Rebecca was born, along with
millions of other Jewish immigrants
from different parts of the world.
These immigrants brought with them
many different traditions and ways
of being Jewish. Practices varied
widely between families, and differ-
ences among Jewish families were
just as common in Rebecca's time as
they are today. Rebecca's stories
show the way one Jewish family
could have lived in 1914 and 1915.

Rebecca's grandparents spoke
mostly *Yiddish*, a language that was
common among Jews from Eastern
Europe. For help in pronouncing or
understanding the foreign words
in this book, look in the glossary on
page 78.

TABLE OF CONTENTS

REBECCA'S FAMILY

PAPA
Rebecca's father, an understanding man who owns a small shoe store

MAMA
Rebecca's mother, who keeps a good Jewish home—and a good sense of humor

REBECCA
A lively girl who dreams of becoming an actress

SADIE AND SOPHIE
Rebecca's twin sisters, who like to remind Rebecca that they are fourteen

BENNY AND VICTOR
Rebecca's brothers, who are five and twelve

GRANDPA
*Rebecca's grandfather,
an immigrant from
Russia who carries on
the Jewish traditions*

BUBBIE
*Rebecca's grandmother,
an immigrant from
Russia who is feisty
and outspoken*

MAX
*Mama's cousin, who
leads the exciting life
of an actor*

MRS. BERG
*A woman in Rebecca's
neighborhood who wants
nothing but the best*

LEO BERG
*A conceited boy from
Rebecca's class*

CHAPTER
ONE

—

A SABBATH
SURPRISE

Rebecca Rubin tugged at her wooden doll until the top and bottom pulled apart to reveal a smaller doll nesting inside. There were seven painted dolls in all, each one tucked inside the next. They reminded Rebecca of her family, which numbered exactly seven.

The dolls had belonged to Mama when she was growing up in Russia, long before Rebecca was born. But now the Russian dolls were Rebecca's treasure. She lined them up along the parlor windowsill, behind the sheer curtains.

"Ladies and gentlemen, your attention please!"

said Rebecca to her imaginary audience. Slowly she drew back the curtains and wiggled the doll she thought of as the mother to the front of the windowsill stage.

"It's almost sundown," Rebecca said in a no-nonsense mama voice. "I hope you've all had your baths." She moved the mama closer to one of the smaller dolls. "Beckie, dear," she said sweetly, "you are so grown-up now. Tonight *you* may light the candles."

Rebecca pretended two of the bigger dolls were her older sisters. She moved them to face the mama and squawked in a high voice, "She's not old enough! She's practically a baby!" The two big sister dolls butted into the little Beckie doll, and it wobbled close to the edge of the windowsill.

Rebecca pushed the papa doll until it stood in front of the others. "Well, curl my mustache," she said in a deep voice. "Beckie's not a baby anymore. She knows the Hebrew blessing perfectly. She is certainly old enough to light the candles tonight."

Before Rebecca could make her brother dolls speak, Mama's very real voice broke into her performance.

"Beckie, you'll have to put away your dolls," she called from the kitchen. "It's time to set the table."

"Phooey!" Rebecca said under her breath. She let the curtains fall across her dolls and turned back to the parlor. Extra leaves had been placed in the table to make room for everyone, and Rebecca smoothed the large white tablecloth. She set out two silver candlesticks and placed one white candle in each.

Every Friday, Mama cooked and cleaned all day to prepare for the Sabbath. Bubbie, Rebecca's grandmother, came down from her apartment upstairs to help cook. Before the sun set, the family came

3

together for a special dinner. Friday night was Rebecca's favorite time of the week. *But Mama should let me do something more important than just setting the table,* she thought as she lifted a tall stack of Mama's best dishes from the sideboard.

Mama looked in from the kitchen. "Don't carry too many plates at once!" she cautioned. "And we need one extra tonight."

"Who's coming?" Rebecca asked, adding a plate and dividing the pile in two. Through the doorway, she could see Bubbie frying fish in a black iron pan. Mama and Bubbie glanced at each other, without answering her question.

That made Rebecca even more curious to know who would be sharing their Sabbath dinner. "Who is it, Mama?"

Mama stirred sizzling potatoes and onions as she answered. "My cousin, Moyshe."

Now Rebecca nearly did drop the plates. "The actor?" she asked. She had overheard her parents talking about Moyshe before, but she had never met him. He usually traveled around the country, acting in vaudeville shows, but other times he was out of work and

4

needed to borrow money from Papa. Rebecca had always wondered what an actor was like in real life, when he wasn't onstage. Tonight she would find out.

Rebecca took special care setting the table. She folded the linen napkins so that the crocheted edges were lined up neatly. If a real actor was coming to dinner, she wanted everything to be perfect.

"Sadie! Sophie!" Bubbie called. A few strands of gray hair slipped from her neat bun and framed her round face. She opened the oven door and slid out two braided loaves of *hallah* bread. Bubbie only baked hallah for Friday nights and holidays. Each loaf needed two eggs, and eggs were expensive.

Rebecca's twin sisters hurried in, wearing matching dresses. Sadie's eyes sparkled, and she looked eager to help. Sophie followed behind her.

"Come check if hallah is done," Bubbie instructed them.

"But the loaves are so hot," Sophie complained. She pulled away from the open oven. Sadie wasn't timid at all. She rapped two fingers against the shiny crust. A hollow sound echoed back.

"Done," Sadie announced.

Why doesn't Bubbie ever ask me to check the bread? Rebecca wondered. *Bubbie treats me like a little child!* She pushed past her sisters.

"I can do it, too," she said.

"So, give a tap," Bubbie told her. "When dough is done, bread sounds empty."

As Rebecca knocked on the bread with her knuckles, her older brother, Victor, sneaked up and rapped on her head. "Done!" he teased. The twins giggled.

Rebecca tried to swat Victor's arm, but before she could catch him, a rhythmic knock sounded at the kitchen door. Everyone turned to stare as it creaked open. A tall young man wearing a jaunty straw hat and holding a polished cane poked his head into the room.

"Moyshe!" Mama exclaimed.

The man put his finger to his lips, signaling everyone to be quiet, and began sprinkling something in the doorway. Rebecca couldn't see anything in his hand. Her little brother, Benny, squatted down. He looked at the floor, and then up at Moyshe.

"What you are putting on this clean floor?" Bubbie cried.

Moyshe peered into the hallway and looked around nervously. Then he made more frantic sprinkling motions. Finally, he spoke. "It's lion powder," he said solemnly.

Rebecca frowned. "What in the world is that?"

"Why, don't you know?" Moyshe asked. "It keeps the lions away."

Benny's eyes grew wide. "Lions?"

Sadie sniffed. "That's ridiculous. There aren't any lions around here."

"You see how well it works!" Moyshe announced.

Benny heaved a sigh of relief. Sadie and Sophie shook their heads at the silly joke. Rebecca burst out laughing.

Moyshe flashed a gleaming smile. "At least one person in this audience likes my joke," he said. "If you make them laugh, your audience will love you." He winked at Rebecca. "Remember that!"

Rebecca had never imagined that Mama's cousin would be so exciting. He even looked interesting, with his bright dark eyes and the cane draped over his arm.

"Come in and close the door, Moyshe," Mama said.

"Excuse me, but it's no more Moyshe Shereshevsky," her cousin said. "I am Max Shepard, if you please." He gave a low bow, sweeping his hat off his head. "An American name for an American actor."

"America," Bubbie grumbled. "Always changing with the names. You don't change a name like a dirty shirt!"

Max didn't argue. "You must be little Beckie," he said, giving Rebecca his full attention. "You were toddling around like a windup doll the last time I saw you. Now you're a young lady!"

Rebecca beamed. Visitors never talked to her first when they met the family—they always fussed over Sadie and Sophie because they thought twins were so remarkable. If only they knew how left out Rebecca felt, being their younger sister!

Max turned to Benny. "And you weren't even born! Now you're old enough to grow buttons."

"Buttons don't grow!" Benny said.

Max pulled something from Benny's ear. "This sure looks like a button to me."

Benny's eyes grew wide as Max dropped a shiny brown button into his hand. Rebecca chuckled. How did Max do it?

"And this must be the *Bar Mitzvah* boy!" Max exclaimed, shaking Victor's hand. "Your mother tells me you're almost thirteen now, and studying hard for your Bar Mitzvah." He dropped his voice lower, as if sharing a secret. "But I hear sneaking out to play baseball is a lot more fun than studying Hebrew." Victor grinned.

Hebrew

"Good *Shabbos!*" Rebecca's grandfather called as he and Papa came in. Grandpa and Bubbie often mixed Yiddish words with their English. Yiddish was the language most Jewish immigrants in the neighborhood spoke. Rebecca could speak it, too, and she knew Shabbos meant Sabbath.

Papa handed Mama a penny bouquet of flowers, as he did every Friday. "Almost as pretty as you," he smiled. Mama blushed at the compliment as she hung her apron on a nail by the stove.

"Good evening, Moyshe," Papa said, shaking hands.

"Excuse me, but that's Max," Bubbie corrected him. "There is no more Moyshe."

Max grinned. "Moyshe, Max, what's the

9

difference? You can call me anything, as long as you don't call me late for dinner!"

Rebecca thought Max was funny. He was nothing like Papa, who was usually so serious.

"Such a busy day at the shoe store," Grandpa said. "But now it's Shabbos, and time to rest."

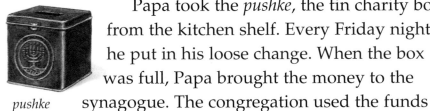

Papa took the *pushke*, the tin charity box, from the kitchen shelf. Every Friday night he put in his loose change. When the box was full, Papa brought the money to the

pushke synagogue. The congregation used the funds they collected to help new immigrants. Papa dropped in the coins from his pocket, and they clanged to the bottom.

Grandpa added some change. "We must always help those who are less fortunate," he said. He held the box out to Max, but just at that moment Max stepped into the parlor and started tickling Benny until he was screaming with laughter.

"Don't make him wild," Mama scolded. "Come, it's time to light the candles."

Benny dashed to Papa and pulled at his sleeve. "My turn! My turn!"

Papa lifted Benny in the air, and he squealed

with delight. "Women light the Shabbos candles," Papa said.

"No fair!" Benny whined.

"Can't I light them tonight?" Rebecca begged. "I know the prayer by heart."

"You heard Papa," Sadie said. "It's for the *women* in the family."

Rebecca frowned. This was just like her windowsill play!

"The twins will light the candles," Mama said firmly. "After all, they're fourteen."

"And not married yet?" Max joked. "Time to call the matchmaker!" The twins put their hands over their mouths and tried to stifle their giggles.

Rebecca went to the windowsill and poked the big sister dolls so hard, they rocked a little. "When will *I* get to light the candles?" she muttered. "The twins get to do *everything!*"

"Stop pouting and help," Bubbie ordered. She set a soup tureen on the sideboard and ladled golden chicken soup into bowls. Rebecca served Max first. He closed his eyes and breathed deeply, as if smelling a sweet perfume.

The family waited while Bubbie hung her apron

 in the kitchen. Then she sat down and straightened the lacquer pin she often wore. It was a keepsake she had brought with her from Russia. Rebecca had always loved the picture of the leaping hare that was painted on the pin's shiny black background. The picture was from a Russian folktale called Clever Karina.

Sadie and Sophie stood before the silver candlesticks. Everyone watched as they lit the white candles with a long wooden match. Then they closed their eyes and recited the Hebrew prayer together, giving thanks for the Sabbath, a day of rest and peace. The candles flickered, lighting up the twins' faces with a golden glow.

"Beautiful," Max murmured. The grown-ups nodded approvingly, and Rebecca felt a bubble of envy grow in her chest. She was old enough to do more than just set the table!

Victor raised the special cup of Sabbath wine and recited the Hebrew blessing. Grandpa corrected his pronunciation, and Rebecca felt secretly pleased. Next, Mama removed the delicately embroidered hallah cover from the warm bread. She held up the two loaves, and the whole family gave thanks for their food. Rebecca said the prayer loudly so that everyone would know *she* didn't make mistakes.

Rebecca sipped her steaming soup, with Mama's homemade noodles. She loved the foods that made Friday nights special. But tonight she wasn't thinking about dinner. An idea was flickering in her mind, forming a glow as bright as the Sabbath candles.

A SHOWY
DINNER

Mama set platters of food on the table,
and Max spooned out a big helping of
potatoes. "There's a new play coming
to the Yiddish theater," he announced.

"Such a long time it's been since we see a play!"
Grandpa said.

"We don't want to see Yiddish plays," Sadie
said. "We like moving pictures." As usual, Sophie
didn't say a word, but she nodded in agreement.

"Moving pitch-es," Grandpa said in his thick
accent. "Why you want to see people moving in
pitch-es, when you can see real people moving
onstage?"

"Movies are smooth," Sophie said. "We're going

14

to see a show tomorrow with our friends."

Grandpa seemed puzzled. "What is this *smooth?*"

"It means modern and exciting!" said Sadie.

Rebecca could only imagine what a moving picture looked like. She had seen posters advertising the newest movies, but she had never been to one. "Can I come?" she asked.

The twins stopped their spoons in midair. With one voice they replied, "You're not old enough."

"You always leave me out," Rebecca argued.

"We're in high school," Sadie reminded her, as if Rebecca hadn't heard that a thousand times.

"There's plenty of time for that nonsense when you're older," Papa declared. "I don't think these new movie pictures are meant for children."

Rebecca fumed. The twins got to do everything together. Even at night, they whispered under their covers while her bed stood alone on the opposite side of the room.

Victor glanced at Grandpa with an impish grin and then turned to Benny. "Speaking of pitch-es," he said to his brother, "how about catching baseballs for me tomorrow afternoon?"

Benny wiggled with excitement. "I can get the ball even if it rolls under the fence!"

The twins are best friends, and Victor and Benny can play ball together, Rebecca thought, *but I have only myself. I'm always left out, even on Friday nights.*

Rebecca thought of her friend Rose. She had her own candlesticks and lit the candles beside her mother every Sabbath. *If I had some candlesticks of my own,* Rebecca thought, *Mama would have to let me light candles.* Her idea began to glow more brightly. She could stand right next to Sadie and Sophie. Then they'd see she was old enough to perform the ceremony, and even old enough to go to the movies!

"I heard the Boston Red Sox have a new player," Max said, taking two crispy pieces of fish. "His name's Babe Ruth."

"Babe?" Bubbie scowled. "This is a name?"

"I read about him in the paper," Victor said importantly. "They say he's going to be an ace pitcher. I wish he was playing for the Yankees."

"If he's good," Max said, "maybe we'll sign him next year."

"Enough about baseball," Papa said. "Now that

16

school has started, I want to hear how my children are doing."

"In English class, we're reading a play called *Hamlet*," Sadie announced.

"It's by William Shakespeare," Sophie added softly.

Max looked pleased. "Ahh—the very best of theater."

Rebecca butted in. Why should her sisters get all the attention? "I got one hundred and ten percent on my arithmetic test," she announced, looking directly at Papa. "Miss Maloncy gave us an extra credit problem, and I even got that right."

"Doing well in school is indeed something to be proud of," Mama said gently, "but be careful not to boast." She wagged her finger at the children. "You don't realize how lucky you are. In Russia, we never had the chance to go to school."

Max nodded in agreement. "Life was hard growing up in Russia. But I have fond memories, too." He lightly touched Bubbie's pin with the picture of the leaping hare. "I remember my mother telling me the story of Clever Karina."

Rebecca knew the story well, as Mama had often

told it at bedtime. Max began telling the tale, his
deep voice as silky as a singer crooning a tune.

"One morning, a poor farmer was overjoyed to
see his horse had given birth to a foal. It was
sleeping under a hay wagon in his neighbor's field.
His wealthy neighbor said, 'Everyone
knows a newborn rests beneath
its mother. Since my hay wagon
is obviously the mother, that
handsome foal is mine.'"

"That's a-diculous!" Benny declared, and
everyone chuckled.

Max went on, telling how the poor man told his
only child, Karina, what had happened. Rebecca was
drawn into the story. She imagined she was little
Karina, trying to help. Acting the role, she said in a
sweet voice, "Go to the tsar, Father, and ask him to
settle the matter."

Max gave Rebecca a broad smile. He reached
for Mama's flowered shawl and draped it around
Rebecca's head. Now she truly felt as if she was in
a play, acting the role of Karina.

Max continued. "But when the tsar heard the
story, he did not make a decision. Instead he posed a

riddle. The tsar said to the two men, 'You must each bring your youngest daughter to me, but she must not come on foot nor on horseback. She must not wear clothes, but she must not be naked. She must not bring a present, but she must come with a gift. The one who solves my riddle will keep the foal.'"

"Phooey on the tsar!" Grandpa scoffed.

"The poor farmer trudged home," said Max, "and told his daughter of the impossible riddle. But Clever Karina knew just what to do."

Rebecca acted out Karina's solution as Max told the end of the tale. "So Karina wrapped herself in her father's fishnet and rode off to the tsar's palace on the back of a giant hare. In her hand she carried a partridge in a cage. When she arrived before the tsar, Karina held up the birdcage."

Rebecca lifted her hand, looking determined. "Here is a gift, Your Majesty," she said, and she pretended to open a latch on a cage. Her hands made a graceful flapping motion, as if a bird were flying away.

"The tsar was pleased with Karina's clever solution to his riddle and decreed that her father should keep the foal. When Karina grew up, the tsar

Rebecca pretended to open a latch on a cage. Her hands made a
graceful flapping motion, as if a bird were flying away.

married her, for he knew he could never find another wife who was nearly as clever."

Max took Rebecca's hand, and she bowed with him as the family clapped. "What an actress!" Max exclaimed. "Our Beckie's a natural talent."

Rebecca could barely breathe. Max thought she was a good actress—and her whole family was clapping for her!

"I'm auditioning for a movie studio this week," Max said. "Maybe I should bring Beckie along!"

Bubbie rolled her eyes. "Don't give her crazy ideas," she said.

Grandpa slapped the table. "Acting is a no-good life for a young lady!"

"Beckie should be a teacher," Papa said, sitting back comfortably. He seemed quite pleased with this idea.

Rebecca's shoulders slumped. Why didn't Papa think she should become an actress? After all, Max said she had talent.

Papa turned to Victor, ending the discussion. "How about working in the store tomorrow?" he asked.

"Tomorrow he comes with me to synagogue,"

Grandpa declared. He turned to Victor and said sternly, "So close to your Bar Mitzvah, your Hebrew is not so good!"

Bubbie shook her head at Papa. "Working on Shabbos," she sighed. "Such a shame."

Rebecca knew Jews weren't supposed to work on Saturday, the day of rest. Grandpa worked at the store all week, but on Saturdays he prayed at the synagogue and often took Victor with him.

"I don't like to work on Shabbos, but most people shop on Saturday. I have to keep the store open if it's going to support the family," Papa said.

Maybe I can't light the candles or go to a movie, Rebecca thought, *but I can help in Papa's store. Then he'll see how grown-up I am.* If she did a good job, maybe Papa would give her a few pennies. That would help her save for candlesticks.

"I'll work tomorrow," she offered.

"I do need help," Papa said. He stroked his mustache thoughtfully. "Why don't we try it?" Rebecca brightened. "Wear your best shoes," he added.

Max sipped his glass of tea. "What do you hear from your brother Jacob in Russia?" he asked Papa.

"Now that Russia is fighting against Germany, they are drafting more men. You know the Russian army takes Jewish boys as young as twelve," Max added. "Jacob's family better get out before the war gets worse."

Lines of worry creased Papa's forehead. "Things are not good," he sighed. He took a letter from his pocket. "This came from Jacob today." He read the letter, changing it into English.

"Dear Brother, I write to tell you that life here is becoming more dangerous as the war spreads. Jews are no longer allowed to work, and I have lost my job. I am afraid to let Josef and Michael out of the house for fear soldiers will snatch them off the street and force them into the tsar's army. Food is scarce, and we are thankful when we have a bit of cabbage soup. Little Ana is sick and weak from hunger, and I fear she will not survive another winter here. A friend will try to smuggle us out of Russia, but it will take every *kopek* we have left. We beg you to send us ship tickets as soon as possible, so we can join you in New York. Our hearts are filled with sorrow, knowing the hardship this expense will cause, but we cannot wait any longer."

kopeks

23

Victor's eyes had a faraway look, and Rebecca wondered if he was imagining life in the Russian army. She was glad Victor didn't have to worry about that. Grandpa had said that Jewish boys were treated harshly and given the most dangerous army jobs. Many boys never saw their families again.

"It's no good in the Old Country," Grandpa said. "From now on, we fill the pushke for family."

Max cleared his throat and looked embarrassed. "I wish I could help," he said, "but I can barely pay for the room I'm renting. Somehow, you've got to send them tickets right away."

"I know," Papa said irritably. "We've been trying to save enough for a long time."

Sophie looked up. "You don't have to give us our allowance every week," she offered.

Rebecca couldn't imagine what it was like not to have enough food to eat. She looked at the dishes on the table. They were empty only because her family had eaten as much as they wanted. Rebecca felt ashamed. She couldn't spend money on candlesticks when her cousin was starving.

"I have a little bit saved, Papa," she said. "Maybe that will help buy the tickets."

Papa shook his head. "Don't worry, children. We need much more than your pennies. I'll find a way to raise the money."

✧

In bed that night, Sadie and Sophie talked until they fell asleep, but Rebecca lay awake thinking about her cousin. Ana must be so frightened. What if she became too sick to escape? The journey from Russia would be long and dangerous. If only Uncle Jacob's family could make it to New York, Rebecca thought, Ana could be like a sister to her. Ana was exactly her age. Why, it would be just like having a twin.

Rebecca could hear Mama and Papa talking softly in the kitchen. "The ship tickets cost at least thirty dollars each, and we need to buy five of them. All our savings won't be enough," Papa said. "And Jacob must have twenty-five dollars in his pocket to get into America." There was a long silence. Rebecca added up the numbers in her head. Papa needed one hundred seventy-five dollars! How would he ever do it?

Rebecca crept out of bed and opened her trunk.

She took out the knotted handkerchief that held
her savings and quietly counted. All she had was
twenty-seven cents. Maybe she should give all
the money to Papa. But it wasn't nearly enough to
buy even one ship ticket. And Papa had said he
didn't want her savings.

Her wooden dolls lay strewn about in the trunk
where she had tossed them after dinner. She put
them back together, each doll nestled safely inside
the next, but she held Beckie close as she snuggled
under the covers.

"Am I being selfish to want candlesticks for
myself?" Rebecca asked her doll. In the dim light
from the kitchen, she could barely see Beckie's
painted smile before she fell asleep.

C H A P T E R
T H R E E

ONE FOR
THE MONEY

Rebecca studied the picture on the
cover of her sisters' movie magazine.
Then she looked again at her own
reflection in the mirror that hung in the parlor. She
tilted the brim of her hat until it slanted across her
forehead. That was just how the movie star Pearl
White wore her hat. Rebecca turned her face to
one side and then the other, admiring the look. She
imagined she was on a movie poster. "Coming Soon!
Rebecca Rubin in *The Perils of Pauline!*"

"Stop primping," Mama called. "You'll make
Papa late."

"I'm coming!" Rebecca smoothed her cotton
stockings and straightened the velvet collar and

cuffs on her dress. Mama always called it her "burgundy" dress, but Rebecca preferred the elegant description from the mail-order catalog: "Rich garnet tweed," it read, "for the sophisticated young lady." Rebecca spit on her finger and rubbed the toes of her black leather shoes to a shine.

Mama held out the leftover hallah from last night. "Take this up to Bubbie," she said. "Grandpa can have it with his lunch."

"But I'm late," Rebecca complained, running up the stairs two at a time. Through the window on the  landing, she glimpsed empty clotheslines strung from the fire escapes. Her Jewish neighbors didn't wash clothes on Saturday. That would be work!

Rebecca opened Bubbie's door and set the bread on the shiny oilcloth that covered the small kitchen table. Sadie and Sophie were in the parlor arguing about how many embroidered napkins they had to make for their wedding chests.

"Napkins, doilies, pillowcases, aprons, tablecloths," Bubbie began, counting on her fingers. "If you don't make them now, you won't have enough linens ready when you start your own home."

"Nobody makes a trousseau anymore, Bubbie," Sadie grumbled. "It's 1914 already, and in America you don't need a trunkful of handmade linens to get married!"

Bubbie came into the kitchen holding the calico bag Rebecca used for her crocheting. "You left your needlework here," she said.

Rebecca tucked the bag under her arm. "Maybe if it gets slow in the shoe store, I'll make another doily."

Bubbie frowned. "I don't think you should crochet on Shabbos—even crocheting is work."

"I'm already helping in the store," Rebecca reasoned.

Bubbie sighed. "I suppose it couldn't be worse," she admitted.

"You'd better take the pattern book," Sadie said. "You'll need the directions."

"I know them by heart," Rebecca said, turning to go.

Bubbie pinched her cheek. "Such a talent with the crochet hook!" She called to the twins, "Your younger sister makes more than both of you for her wedding chest."

"Bully for her," Sadie scoffed.

Rebecca raced down the steps and out the front door. *If I'm old enough to prepare for my wedding,* she thought, *why aren't I old enough to go to the movies or light the candles?*

Papa stood on the sidewalk, tapping his foot. Rebecca had wanted the day to be perfect, and already she had spoiled things by being late!

"Sorry, Papa," she began, "I had to fix my hat, and then—"

"My, how dramatic!" Papa smiled, looking at the tilted brim. "So, today you'll be my stylish helper." He put his arm around her shoulder as they walked down East Seventh Street. Papa kept a quick pace, and Rebecca hurried to keep up.

"We'll save a little money and skip the trolley," he said. "But we won't save time. It's a long walk."

If Papa didn't want Rebecca's savings, why did he need to save the five-cent fare for the trolley? She tried not to think about the money they needed for cousin Ana and her family. Rebecca had saved so little—how could she make a difference?

Marigolds bloomed in the window boxes on the row houses in Rebecca's neighborhood. As she and

30

Papa walked, the streets became
narrower, and storefronts looked out
from the ground floor of tenement
buildings. They crossed the busy
thoroughfare of East Houston Street,
and Rebecca admired the elegant window displays
in the shops. At last they turned onto Rivington
Street. Instead of the usual weekday bustle, just a
few pushcarts lined the road. Pungent
smells of pickles and cheese and
herring filled the air. Neighbors passed
each other on the street, and Rebecca
heard greetings in many different
languages.

When she saw the familiar blue awning of Papa's
shoe store, she dashed across the street. Papa caught
up to her, out of breath.

"Slow down! You have to watch for wagons,
and now there are automobiles, too. Those reckless
drivers don't look out for little girls."

Rebecca just grinned and reached for the key in
Papa's hand. "Let me do it!" She unlocked the front
door and the bell on top jingled cheerily, as if to
welcome her. She stepped inside and hung a sign in

the window. It said OPEN in English, Yiddish, and Italian. Rebecca hung her hat and shawl in the back room and put her calico bag next to a row of shoe boxes.

"I'll start dusting," she offered, taking the feather duster from its hook. She wanted Papa to see that she could be a big help.

Rebecca breathed in the thick, buttery smell of new leather. She loved the way the shoes sat at attention on the narrow shelves as if they were waiting for the chance to march outside. She whisked the dust from the shoes on display, singing as she worked.

"Take me out to the ball game," she sang. "Take me out with the crowd…" In the children's area, she brushed lightly over tiny high-topped boots, thick-soled play shoes, and dainty dress shoes with straps that buttoned across the ankle. "Buy me some peanuts and Cracker Jack, I don't care if I never get back!" She dusted women's shoes with pointy toes, fancy buckles, and squashed heels.

"If the ball game is over," Papa joked, "the sidewalk needs sweeping." He handed Rebecca a tattered broom. "The pushcart peddlers leave such a mess Friday afternoon. I have to sweep up so the store looks better. Put on my workshop apron so your dress won't get dirty."

Rebecca wrinkled her nose. She didn't want to put the stained canvas apron over her beautiful dress. Then Papa handed her a pair of worn leather boots. "Wear these instead of your good shoes," he told her. Rebecca started to argue, but she didn't want to annoy Papa. She tied on the big apron and replaced her shiny shoes with the old boots.

Outside, Rebecca consoled herself by pretending she was auditioning for the movie studio with Max. She imagined she was playing a poor immigrant who had to sweep the streets to help her family survive. She pushed the broom slowly to show how exhausted she was. She swept up banana peels, soggy potatoes, and pieces of newspaper blowing against the curb. *Life in America is so hard,* she pretended. *I can't go to school but must work every day for pennies!* She hummed a sad Yiddish song.

Lost in her playacting, Rebecca was startled by Leo Berg, a pesky boy from her class at school. His mother walked beside him. An elegant fur scarf was draped around her neck, ending in a fox's head, tail, and paws that dangled from her shoulders. Mrs. Berg swished inside the shoe store without a glance, but Leo stared at Rebecca while she swept.

"This is my father's store," Rebecca said proudly. "I'm helping today."

"Why, you're nothing but a street sweeper," Leo sniffed, brushing at his jacket.

Imagining she was a poor sweeper in a movie was fine, Rebecca thought, but having someone call her one was unbearable! Her face burned with anger.

"Sweeping the sidewalk is very important," she declared. "Maybe if you knew how to work hard,

you wouldn't have to wear the dunce cap in school."

Leo's cheeks turned red. "You'd better be polite, or my mother and I will leave!" He stepped inside, slamming the door so hard that the glass pane rattled.

dunce cap

How could she keep quiet when Leo had insulted her? Yet Rebecca couldn't let Papa lose a customer. She swept harder and faster, pushing her anger around with the dirt.

When she finished, she walked straight to the

"Why, you're nothing but a street sweeper," Leo sniffed.

back room and put on her own shoes. As she hung up Papa's apron, she could hear Leo complaining. Rebecca peeked through the curtains that screened off the back room.

"These shoes are ugly!" Leo grumbled.

"We've been to every shoe store on Broadway," Mrs. Berg said. "Leopold didn't like anything!"

Papa sat on a low stool, helping Leo take off a pair of shoes. Open boxes and loose shoes were strewn around the floor. Instead of looking cross, Papa just smiled. "I might have to show you a special pair I've been saving." He hesitated. "I don't know if I should. These shoes aren't for any ordinary boy."

"*I'm* not an ordinary boy," Leo piped up. "What's so special about them?"

Papa rubbed his chin. "Well," he began, "these shoes are made of the same leather used for cowboy boots."

"I want to try them!" Leo demanded. "I see cowboy boots in Western movies every week."

Rebecca fumed. Leo was her age, and he saw movies every week!

"Oh, do show us the shoes, Mr. Rubin," Leo's mother said. "I'm at my wit's end! If Leopold likes them, I don't care what they cost."

Papa came into the storage room and searched the boxes stacked according to style and size.

"Cowboy boot leather?" Rebecca whispered.

Papa winked. "Boots or shoes, leather is leather," he said.

Rebecca took her bag of crocheting and walked past Leo without glancing in his direction. Sitting near the bright front window, she looped the thick cotton thread around her crochet hook and pulled the stitches through until a lacy flower design took shape.

Mrs. Berg walked around, inspecting the latest women's shoes. "My, my," she clucked. "Aren't you the clever girl! I didn't know anyone still learned to crochet now that so few young ladies make a trousseau." She picked up a satiny shoe with silk bows.

Rebecca wondered if Sadie and Sophie were right. Maybe girls didn't make linens for their wedding chests anymore. She held her doily higher so that Mrs. Berg could admire it. "Well, I'm only nine and I'm not planning to get married for a long time," Rebecca explained. "But I learned to crochet when I was six, and Bubbie says I have a knack for it."

"That's enough, Rebecca," said Papa. "Let Mrs. Berg browse in peace."

Rebecca pursed her lips. Once again, she had talked too much. If Papa found out what she had said to Leo about the dunce cap, he might send her home!

Mrs. Berg peered closely at the doily. "You couldn't buy such a fine piece for love or money."

Rebecca swelled with pride. Leo's mother was a lot nicer than Leo was. Feeling generous, she took a finished doily from her bag and handed it to Mrs. Berg. "Please take this one," she offered. "I've made so many."

Mrs. Berg patted Rebecca on the head. "What a sweet child." She folded the doily into her purse. "I will certainly enjoy displaying it in our new home. We're moving uptown in the spring, you know."

With a dramatic rustle of tissue paper, Papa unwrapped the shoes. He sniffed the leather. "Ah, the aroma of saddles and boots," he said.

Rebecca fought back a giggle. Why, Papa was an actor, too!

Leo grabbed one of the shoes and smelled it.

"All right," Papa said, "try them. But they might not fit." He eased Leo's foot into the shoe with a shiny brass shoehorn.

"They're perfect for me," Leo announced. He put on the second shoe and laced it up himself. Then he tucked his thumbs into the waist of his knickers and strutted around the room with his chest out.

"Doesn't he look handsome in those shoes!" gushed Mrs. Berg. "He'll wear them home."

"Shall I wrap up the old ones?" Papa asked.

"No," Leo said. "Get rid of them."

Papa went to the cash register, and Rebecca began replacing all the shoes in their proper boxes. She hoped Papa would notice how neat everything was.

As Mrs. Berg swept toward the door, she bent down and handed Rebecca something. The bell on the door jingled them out, and Rebecca saw a shiny quarter in her hand. Mrs. Berg had paid her for the doily! She didn't want Papa to see. He might tell her to return the money. Her heart thumped as she hid the quarter in her bag and picked up Leo's old shoes.

"What shall I do with these, Papa? They're hardly scuffed."

"They will be put to good use," Papa said.

"Set them on the workbench."

Rebecca carried a stack of shoe boxes into the back, along with Leo's old shoes. As she placed his shoes on the workbench, she saw several other pairs of worn children's shoes lined up near cans of shoe polish. The bench was littered with tools, tiny nails, and scraps of leather.

"What will you do with these old shoes, Papa?" she asked.

Jing-jing! The bell on the door announced a customer before he could answer. A thin woman with dark braids pinned up around her head stepped inside. A small boy held her hand.

"May I help you?" Papa asked.

"My son's shoes, they are too small," she said in a heavy Italian accent. "A friend says to me you have shoes not cost too much?"

"Sit down," Papa smiled. The boy was about the same age as Benny. He had on a pair of worn knickers, and his stockings were mended around the knees. Papa pushed his thumb against the toe of the boy's shoe. "Definitely a bit snug." He took off the old shoes, and Rebecca saw that the soles were worn all the way through. Papa measured the boy's feet with a wooden measuring slide.

"You'd think my little Joey would have plenty shoes," the woman said, "since his father works in shoe factory."

Papa nodded. "I worked in a shoe factory when I first came here from Russia, and I never had a decent pair of my own. I had to put cardboard in my shoes so my socks wouldn't rub the sidewalk!" Papa picked up the boy's old shoes and said, "Let me see what I can do with these."

Rebecca counted out her stitches, her crochet hook darting in and out. When the boy looked over his shoulder at her, she winked. He giggled and hid his head in his mother's skirt.

Papa returned holding a polished pair of shoes. "I've fixed them up so they hardly look like the same pair." He slipped the boy's feet into the shoes.

"Look, I can wiggle my toes," Joey exclaimed. He skipped around the store.

Rebecca squinted at the shoes as Joey went by. "They certainly *don't* look like the same pair," she remarked, but Papa's stern look silenced her. Why wasn't she supposed to say what was plain as day?

She lowered her eyes and moved only her fingers instead of her mouth.

"How much I owe you?" the woman asked.

"Not a penny," Papa said. "I just fixed his shoes up a bit."

"I thank you so much," the woman said with a grateful smile.

Papa patted the boy's shoulder. "Wear them in good health, Joey." Rebecca watched Joey set off down the street, hopping over cracks in the sidewalk.

"Now you know why I save the old shoes," Papa said quietly. "I keep them for situations just like this."

"Does the lady know what you did?" Rebecca asked.

Papa nodded. "She knows. But it's best not to talk about it, Beckie. No one likes to take charity."

"That was a good thing to do, Papa," said Rebecca. She gave him a hug.

"It's a *mitzvah*," Papa explained. "We should help others whenever we can. Your heart tells you the right thing to do. But you already know that, don't you?"

Rebecca felt a twinge in her own heart as she remembered Ana. Shouldn't she be doing something to help her cousin?

The store grew busier, and thoughts of Ana soon disappeared. As Rebecca carried boxes back and forth, she remembered the quarter in her bag. What if she brought more doilies to the store next week? Maybe Mrs. Berg would come back.

"Papa, could I work with you every Saturday?" she asked.

"We'll see," Papa said. "We'll see."

TWO FOR THE SHOW

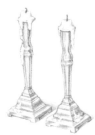

On Sunday afternoon, Rebecca stood at the kitchen sink, trying to clean melted wax from the candlesticks. *Why should I have to clean these,* she thought grumpily, *when I can't even light the candles?*

She scraped at the wax with her fingernail, wondering how much more money she would need to buy her own candlesticks. With the quarter from Mrs. Berg, she had saved just fifty-two cents. Even if she bargained with the peddlers, that wouldn't be enough. Candlesticks would cost at least two dollars.

She thought again of Ana, and her stomach fluttered. Lighting candles wasn't as important as having enough food to eat. Should she give her savings to Papa for the ship tickets? But Papa had already refused her money and told her not to worry. He would get the tickets soon, wouldn't he?

"'To be, or not to be: that is the question,'" floated a voice from the girls' bedroom. Sadie and Sophie were reading *Hamlet* aloud to each other.

To buy, or not to buy, Rebecca thought. *That is* my *question!*

"Vroom! Rrroom!" Benny ran around the parlor holding a toy airplane aloft.

"*Shah!*" Papa hushed him. "Your sisters are studying." He turned the page of his newspaper.

Rebecca walked into the parlor as she polished the gleaming candlesticks with a clean cloth. Through the open window, she could see people strolling along the sidewalks in the mild September air. Neighbors sat on their front stoops, talking and laughing. Victor was off playing stickball, and Mama had gone out. Rebecca didn't want to stay inside tiptoeing around.

She could hear Sadie and Sophie reading Shakespeare's lines with great feeling. But they didn't have an audience, as she'd had when she acted out the folktale with Max. Thinking about performing gave Rebecca an idea. People paid money to see a show! Sometimes children tap-danced right on Orchard Street, between the peddlers' carts, and shoppers tossed pennies to them.

Rebecca took Mama's summer straw hat from its hook and put it on. Its wide, floppy brim and big pink flowers would get people's attention. She rolled up a black wool scarf and draped it around her neck like Mrs. Berg's fur.

"I'm going out," she called to Papa from the kitchen. She hoped he wouldn't look up from his paper. Rebecca hurried to the door, but she wasn't quick enough.

"Me, too!" Benny demanded, landing his plane on one of Mama's geraniums.

"Take him with you," Papa ordered, "so the twins can study."

Rebecca's heart sank. Taking Benny would ruin her plan. But her brother happily pulled his bag of marbles from a box on the kitchen floor. He grabbed his cap and ran down the steps.

The front stoop of their row house was empty.

46

The carved lions' heads on each side of
the door looked down with a silent roar.
Rebecca saw the sidewalk below her.
Why, the stoop is just like a stage, she thought.

"I'm going to put on a show," she said to
her brother. "So just stay out of the way."

"I want to be in a show, too," Benny said.

Rebecca thought for a moment. If she didn't let
Benny help out, he would just keep bothering her.
"Tell you what—you can play the organ grinder's
monkey," she told him. "You go into the
crowd and pass your hat around to collect
pennies."

Benny started screeching like a monkey
and hopping from one foot to the other.

"This is fun!" he cried. "But where's
the crowd?"

"We haven't started the show yet," Rebecca
explained. "Don't be such a *nudge*, pestering me
every minute."

Rebecca stood at the edge of the stoop, right
at the top of the steps. She took a deep breath and
began singing her favorite song. "Take me out to the
ball game, take me out with the crowd . . ."

47

A few passersby turned to look, but they didn't
stop. Rebecca kept singing. Maybe she just had to be
patient. Surely a crowd would form soon. She sang
louder. But when she finished, no one had stopped,
and there were no pennies in Benny's cap.

Rebecca tilted the floppy brim on Mama's straw
hat at an angle, like Pearl White's hat. She cleared
her throat and began singing at the top of her lungs.

> I went to the animal fair,
> The birds and the beasts were there.
> The big baboon by the light of the moon
> Was combing his auburn hair.

Benny hopped up and down, hooting and
scratching his chest the way the organ grinder's
monkey scratched his fur. A few people paused to
watch as Rebecca belted out the end of the song.

> The monkey he got drunk
> And climbed up the elephant's trunk,
> The elephant sneezed and fell on his knees,
> And what became of the monk,
> The monk, the monk, the monk?

As Rebecca repeated "the monk" over and over, Benny flitted through the thin crowd. Rebecca saw a stout man drop a coin into the hat. Now she was getting somewhere! Maybe a few jokes would bring the people closer. Max had said, "If you make them laugh, your audience will love you."

Rebecca walked down a few steps and began sprinkling the sidewalk with imaginary powder. "Ask me what I'm doing," she whispered to Benny.

"Okay," Benny whispered back. "What are you doing?"

"Louder," Rebecca hissed through her teeth, pretending to look around nervously.

"What are you *doing?*" Benny yelled.

"I'm sprinkling lion powder!" Rebecca announced clearly.

"Lion powder?" asked Benny. "What's that for?"

The crowd drew closer and looked from Rebecca's hand to the steps. More people joined the group.

Rebecca sprinkled with renewed energy. This routine was going well. "Why, it keeps the lions away," she replied loudly.

Benny started laughing, and Rebecca had to prompt him with the next line. But Benny was quick. "I 'member," he insisted. "But there aren't any lions around here!" he shouted to the crowd. Then he pointed toward the front door. "'Cept for those ones up there!" The audience chuckled. Benny was a little showman.

Rebecca delivered the punch line. "Well, then, you see how well it works!"

People began to laugh. Benny jumped into the gathering holding out his hat, and Rebecca heard the clink of coins. Suddenly, strong fingers pinched her ear.

"Youch!" she cried. She twisted around and saw Bubbie, who was furiously pulling her up the steps.

"You are shaming us in the neighborhood," Bubbie scolded. "Even Mr. Rossi sees you begging!" Rebecca caught a glimpse of the man in the basement apartment scowling at her through his window as Bubbie dragged her along.

"Let go," Rebecca pleaded. "What did I do wrong?"

"You get inside and think about it!" Bubbie said.

"Why is it okay for Max to earn money in a show, but it's not okay for me?"

"Max, Schmax!" Bubbie sputtered. "He doesn't

*Benny jumped into the gathering holding out his hat,
and Rebecca heard the clink of coins.*

earn two nickels to rub together. Such a man you don't want to be like!"

But Rebecca really *did* want to be a performer, just like Max. She couldn't see anything wrong with earning money by putting on a show.

Rebecca saw her brother pulling out his marbles. His cap was still on the sidewalk. "Benny," she hissed under her breath. "Bring the cap!"

Bubbie led Rebecca into the girls' bedroom and left, closing the door firmly behind her. Sadie and Sophie looked up from *Hamlet*.

"You're not ready for the stage yet," Sadie laughed, "but the hat is really you!"

Rebecca's cheeks felt hot. "People liked my show," she said. "They even paid for it!" she added as Benny burst into the room and dumped the pennies on her bed. She counted six copper coins. It wasn't much, but it was something. She tied the money into her handkerchief.

"I want some pennies, too!" Benny protested.

"It was my idea," Rebecca argued, "and my show."

"But I did the joke," Benny insisted. "And I got the pennies." Rebecca dropped a penny into his hand. "No fair!" he whined. "You've got more than me!"

"Oh, all right!" Rebecca gave him two more pennies. It was better than having Bubbie come in to settle it. Benny dashed off, and Rebecca looked dismally at what was left. After all that effort, she had just three cents.

Sadie closed her book with a dull thud that echoed in Rebecca's ears. "We're going to the park. How can anyone study in this madhouse?" A wayward curl at her forehead bounced like a coiled spring. Sophie always plastered her curl flat. It was one way to tell the twins apart.

Rebecca flopped onto her bed. The show had seemed like such a good idea, but Bubbie certainly didn't approve. *Were* the neighbors laughing at her? she wondered. It hardly mattered anyway, since she could never earn much money singing on the stoop. So far, the most she had earned at one time was the quarter she had gotten from Mrs. Berg.

Rebecca buried her pennies in her trunk, pushing aside the neatly folded doilies and linens stored inside. *Imagine saving all these until I'm grown-up*, she thought. She counted the items she had made—ten pillow covers, seventeen doilies, six long table scarves, and twenty-four napkins. She couldn't use all those linens in her whole life! But seeing the piles of needlework gave her another idea. She packed several items into her calico bag until it bulged.

If Papa would just let her work in the store a few more Saturdays, she'd earn all the money she needed. In just a few weeks, she would stand next to her sisters on Friday night and light candles herself. Everyone would see how grown-up she was. Even Bubbie would be proud of her then.

SOLVING
A RIDDLE

A month had passed, and Rebecca had
worked with Papa every Saturday. Today
the store was as busy as ever. Some
customers browsed among the displays, some paid
for their new shoes, and others sat and waited for
Papa to fit them. No wonder he had to keep the
store open on Saturdays.

Each week Rebecca had improved on her plan
to earn money. Now she knew exactly what to do.
While Papa bustled between his customers and the
back room, she draped a few doilies and pillow
covers over a chair. As the ladies strolled by, examining
the latest styles, Rebecca hummed and rearranged
her pieces.

"How lovely," commented a customer. She fingered a lacy table runner, the plumes on her hat swaying. "Now that so few girls make a trousseau, it's hard to find handmade items anywhere. My niece just announced her engagement, and this table runner would be a charming gift. Is it for sale?" the lady asked.

"Oh, no," Rebecca said. "I made these myself, and they take so long!"

The lady pulled a quarter from her purse and held it between her gloved thumb and forefinger. "Would this change your mind, dear?" she asked.

"I couldn't," Rebecca murmured. "Papa might be angry."

"It will be our little secret," the lady whispered as she added a dime.

Rebecca quickly folded the table runner into the customer's shopping bag and tucked the coins into her own bag. As Papa stepped out of the back room with a stack of shoe boxes, the lady put her finger to her lips. Rebecca smiled demurely.

This routine had been repeated many times over the past few Saturdays. She wasn't offering to sell her work, Rebecca told herself. If people insisted on

buying, it wasn't because she had asked them. She
didn't even bargain. She had discovered that people
offered more money if you simply said an item
wasn't for sale. When she brought her calico bag
home each week, it was no longer bulging with
doilies and napkins, but it was heavy with dimes,
quarters, and half-dollars.

Rebecca replaced several pairs of unwanted
shoes in their boxes, smoothed the rumpled tissue
paper, and tried to avoid Papa's eyes. He really
might be angry if he knew what she was doing.
After all, people had come into the store to
buy shoes, and she was taking their attention.

"What a fine helper you have," commented
an elderly man buying a pair of dressy brogues.
"Maybe someday the store will be called 'Rubin and
Daughter.'"

Papa smiled proudly. "No, this young lady is
going to be a teacher."

Maybe, Rebecca thought. *Or I might be an actress.*

Papa placed the man's box of shoes on the glass
case near the cash register. Inside the case were
a few dusty cans of shoe polish and wooden
shoetrees to help shoes keep their shape.

Rebecca thought doilies would be much prettier to display and sell. But how could she tell Papa without giving away her secret?

❧

"You're awfully quiet this evening," Papa said as they walked home. "I guess being a working girl is more tiring than you realized."

But Rebecca wasn't tired. Her plan to sell her linens had worked better than she had expected. Now she had more than enough money to shop for candlesticks on Orchard Street. At first, her heart had skipped at the happy thought. But then she began to worry about whether she should be selling her trousseau. Her trunk was nearly empty now. Bubbie had been so proud of her needle-work—she'd be very upset if she found out Rebecca had sold it.

And something else was bothering her even more. She couldn't stop thinking about Ana, who had to leave Russia soon. How could her cousin make such a long journey when she was weak and ill? Ana would need a lot of courage to face the dangerous escape.

"Papa," she asked, "is cousin Ana still sick? Is she coming to America soon?"

Papa gave her hand a squeeze. "Is that what's on your mind?" he asked. "I'm afraid I haven't heard any more news about Ana. I've been setting aside as much money as possible, but we still need a great deal more. I'll send Uncle Jacob the ship tickets as soon as I can."

Rebecca swallowed, feeling uncertain. The last time she had offered her savings to Papa, he hadn't wanted her pennies. But now she had a lot more than twenty-seven cents. In fact, she thought she had enough for real silver candlesticks. If she used her money to buy them, she could finally light the candles every Friday night. She still wanted to light the candles as much as ever, but somehow the thought of buying her own candlesticks had lost its glow.

Rebecca's hand in Papa's felt hot and sweaty. Papa always said helping others was a mitzvah— something you should do. She remembered the day in the shoe store when Papa had said, "Your heart tells you the right thing to do." Rebecca's heart beat faster in her chest. *Instead of helping Ana, I've been thinking only of myself*, she realized. *I've got to*

"Papa," she asked, "is cousin Ana still sick?
Is she coming to America soon?"

*give Papa the money I've earned so that he can buy the
ship tickets as soon as possible.*

Rebecca was about to make her offer when
a more troubling thought stopped her from saying
a word. Papa would ask where she got the money.
If she told him she had been selling her needlework
in the store, he would be angry. And what would
Bubbie and Mama say when they found out she
had sold her trousseau? Rebecca's throat felt dry.
She could never tell them what she had done!

When Rebecca and Papa turned in at their row
house, Mr. Rossi was washing chalk from
the sidewalk with a long-handled broom.
A bucket of brown water stood in a soapy
puddle near the stoop. Mr. Rossi cleaned
the building in exchange for his rent,
but Rebecca thought he acted as if he owned it.

"These kids is always drawing the chalk
marks!" he complained. He glowered at Rebecca.
"It's you girls making the squares for jumping!"

"*I* wasn't playing hopscotch, Mr. Rossi," Rebecca
said. "I was working at my father's store today."

He wiggled his finger in her face. "Today, is not
you. Tomorrow, maybe *is* you!"

61

What a grouch Mr. Rossi was! He lived alone and didn't like children at all. So what if the neighborhood girls chalked a hopscotch game on the sidewalk? It wasn't *his* sidewalk, thought Rebecca, and besides, the chalk marks would wash away as soon as it rained. But she couldn't waste time worrying about Mr. Rossi. His problem with the chalk wasn't as important as her problem at all.

⚜

All through dinner, thoughts about her empty trunk and Ana and the candlesticks chased each other around in Rebecca's head. Then a horrible thought crept into her mind. Uncle Jacob had said he didn't think Ana could survive another winter. What if her cousin got sicker? What if—what if she died?

I've got to give my money to Papa before it's too late, Rebecca thought. But how could she admit what she had done?

Rebecca barely looked up when there was a rhythmic tapping on the door and Max walked in.

"Moyshe," Grandpa said, "you're too late for dinner, but come sit."

Max lifted the lids off the pans on the
stove. "First I'll help with the leftover
blintzes," he said. "After all, I do want to
help out around here."

blintzes

Mama filled a plate and added a dollop of
sour cream. Max sat down and ate hungrily.

"Do you feel like tea?" Bubbie asked him.

"Well, let me see." Max pinched his arm. "No,
I don't think I do feel like tea. How about Benny?" He
pinched Benny's nose. "Nope, he doesn't feel like tea,
either. As for Beckie," he said, pinching her cheek,
"you don't feel like tea at all. More like a rosy peach."

A murmur of laughter rippled around the table.
Rebecca couldn't even smile. She knew in her heart
what she had to do—but why did it have to be so
hard? She thought again of Ana and the courage it
would take to escape to America. If Rebecca was
going to help her cousin, she would have to show
some courage, too.

She twisted her napkin in her hand. "Papa," she
began in a whispery voice, "I—"

But Max already had Papa's ear. "Believe it or
not, I didn't come by just to sponge a dinner from
you," he said. "I saw a newsreel at the theater today.

The war is spreading fast, and fewer ships are leaving Europe. There's no time to spare if you want to get Jacob and his family out."

Papa scowled. "I know, Max," he snapped. "I'm doing the best I can."

"You don't understand," Max said, pulling a wallet from his pocket. "I really did come here to help." A wide grin spread across his face. "Remember the audition I had a few weeks ago? Well, you are now looking at Max Shepard, movie actor."

Rebecca stared at Max in amazement. Imagine, a movie actor in her family!

Grandpa lifted his bushy eyebrows. "So, it's a good job?"

"The best!" Max said. "I'll be working steady and getting paid every week. In fact, I got my first paycheck yesterday." Bubbie gasped as he pulled five crisp ten-dollar bills from his wallet.

"The movie business pays pretty good dough," Max said. "No more borrowing money for me! I can pay off my debts and look for my own apartment now." Max handed Papa the money. "I hope this helps buy your brother's tickets."

Papa blinked as if he couldn't believe his eyes.

Then he shook his head and tried to give back the money. "You don't have to do this," he said. "After all, it's not your brother."

But Max wouldn't take it. "Consider it repayment for all the money you've loaned me over the years," Max said. He winked at Mama. "And all the dinners you're going to feed me, now that I'm living here in the city."

Papa shook Max's hand and accepted his gift. "This will go a long way," he admitted. "I'll borrow the rest of what we need. It will just take a while to pay it off." Mama leaned over and gave Max a kiss on the cheek.

"And there's one more thing," Max added. "Is it really true that there are people in this family who have yet to see a moving picture?"

"You can put me on that list," Mama said with a smile at Rebecca.

"This is my last weekend working as an usher at the Strand," Max said. "If you come to the matinee tomorrow, I'll get the whole family in free."

Rebecca could barely believe it. There seemed to be no end to Max's surprises.

Bubbie and Grandpa exchanged nervous glances.

"Don't worry," Max reassured them. "It's a Charlie Chaplin comedy, *Dough and Dynamite*. It's perfect for everyone—even Benny. You'll laugh until your sides hurt!" He nudged Rebecca. "And there's an episode of *The Perils of Pauline* with Pearl White."

Charlie Chaplin

How Rebecca had dreamed of seeing a moving picture! But tonight Max's surprise didn't make her happy. When Papa and Mama learned what she had done, they would make her stay home, she was sure. Blinking back tears, Rebecca slipped from the room and returned with her calico bag.

"I have something to tell you, Papa," she said. "Please don't be angry." She took handfuls of change from her bag and dropped them onto the table. Nickels, dimes, quarters, and heavy half-dollars clinked into a pile. Everyone stared at her.

Mama's lips were set in a thin line. "Rebecca Rubin, where did you get this money?"

Rebecca's face burned. She tried not to look at Bubbie. "I—I sold my needlework at the shoe store."

"*Oy vey!*" Bubbie cried. "Your trousseau—such a shame!"

"I'm sorry," Rebecca said, her eyes downcast.

"How did you do it?" asked Sadie.

"I brought my linens and doilies to the store, and ladies offered me money for them." Tears of shame filled Rebecca's eyes.

Mama shook her head slowly, as if she couldn't believe what Rebecca had done. "Why did you do this?" she asked.

Rebecca answered in a near whisper. "I wanted to buy candlesticks."

"For what you need candlesticks?" Bubbie asked. "One pair isn't enough?"

Rebecca hung her head. "*I* wanted to light candles on Shabbos, too."

Everyone sat in silence. Rebecca wished she could make herself disappear.

Then Mama came over and lifted Rebecca's chin. "Always so impatient," she sighed. "I was impatient once, too. I thought I'd never be old enough to welcome the Sabbath. I pretended to light candles using twigs stuck in the ground." She wrapped her arms around Rebecca and held her.

Now that her secret was out, tears of relief and regret rolled down Rebecca's cheeks. "The more

things I sold," she sobbed, "and the more money I earned, the less important the candlesticks seemed."

"So," Papa said, "that's what brought on all the secret deals in the shoe store."

Rebecca blinked in astonishment. "You knew I was selling my things?" she asked. "And you aren't angry?"

Papa shrugged. "When your daughter is a successful American businesswoman, what can a father do except sit back and watch?"

Rebecca wiped her eyes and looked at Papa. "What I really want is for Ana and her family to come. I've got more than eight dollars. I know that's not nearly enough for a ticket, but maybe I could sell some more things, and you won't need to borrow so much money."

Suddenly, Sophie spoke up. Her voice was filled with excitement. "Sadie and I have oodles of napkins and doilies and linens. Let's sell some of those, too!" This time it was Sadie who nodded in agreement, her curl bouncing.

Rebecca's face brightened. "You know, Papa," she said, "the display case near the cash register is wasted with shoe polish in it. Let's put the linens there!"

Bubbie sat silently. Now she looked thoughtful. "If people pay to have doilies," she said, "I have a trunkful. And tablecloths, bed covers, fancy shawls . . . all sitting in a dark trunk. So, I'll sell a little, too! It's a mitzvah."

Grandpa patted Bubbie's arm. "After all, you're already married. A trousseau you don't need!"

For the first time in weeks, Rebecca's heart felt light. Papa didn't mind what she had done. Mama understood why she had sold her needlework. And Bubbie wasn't angry. She was even going to help!

69

"If this works," Papa said, "we'll pay for the tickets in no time." He put his hand on Rebecca's shoulder. "But you, young lady, will have to be in charge of handling the merchandise. Do you think you can arrange the display case?"

"I know I can!" Rebecca exclaimed.

Max stood up. In a deep stage voice he said, "In the true Russian tradition, the youngest daughter has solved the family's riddle of how to get the money for ship tickets." He raised his glass of tea. "Here's to Rebecca!"

Bubbie got up and came over to Rebecca. She unhooked the pin with the leaping hare from her collar and fastened it to Rebecca's dress. "Keep this, to remember that you are our own Clever Karina."

Rebecca hugged Bubbie. "Just as long as I don't have to marry the tsar!" she said.

"Don't worry," Mama laughed. "He'd never have you without a trousseau!"

LOOKING BACK

AMERICA
IN
1914

Hester Street in New York City, where many immigrants lived

When Rebecca was a girl, the United States was growing rapidly. Every year many thousands of *immigrants*, or people who had left their old countries, arrived in America to make new lives. Most of them settled in big cities, where there were plenty of jobs and places to live. Cities often had entire neighborhoods settled by immigrants from one country, such as Italy, Greece, or Russia. There the immigrants had neighbors who spoke their language, and they could buy familiar foods as well as books and newspapers written in the language of their old country.

New York City was the largest city in America,

This shoe shop has signs in Yiddish as well as English.

and its largest group of immigrants was Jews from Russia. At that time, the Russian empire was ruled by the powerful tsar. The tsar did not regard his Jewish subjects as real Russians, because the Jews practiced a different religion and spoke a different language, Yiddish. As a result, Russia had many laws designed to keep its Jewish population living in poverty. Jews were barred from most jobs. They could not own land or travel freely. Jewish boys as young as 12 could be drafted into the tsar's army, where they were treated cruelly and often died. Even worse, Russian soldiers sometimes led *pogroms*, or violent attacks on Jews. They broke into Jewish homes, shops, and temples, looting and burning—and often killing the people inside. They did this out of *prejudice*, the belief that people who are different are bad.

Tsar Nicholas II

Jews like Rebecca's parents and grandparents began leaving Russia and other parts of eastern Europe,

This Jewish family's home was ransacked in a pogrom by Russian soldiers.

This poster reminded immigrants of the conditions they had left in the Old World and the advantages of life in America.

seeking safer countries where their families could lead better lives. Between 1880 and 1914, two million Jews left eastern Europe and came to America. Most of them arrived in New York City, just like Rebecca's family.

Immigrants brought the traditions of their old countries to America. Every Friday evening, Jewish families welcomed the Sabbath with candles and prayers. The Sabbath, which lasted until sundown on Saturday, was supposed to be a day of rest, to honor God's rest on the seventh day of creation. Like Rebecca's papa, however, many Jews had to work on Saturday to feed their families. The immigrants who followed Jewish traditions more strictly, like Bubbie and Grandpa, often disapproved of those who did not. This conflict between old ways and new ways is one that all immigrants face when they move to a new country.

At a Sabbath dinner, special blessings were said over the candles, the hallah loaves, and the cup of wine.

Most of the Jewish immigrants spoke Yiddish, just like Rebecca's grandparents. The children of Jewish immigrants, like Rebecca and her sisters and brothers, grew up speaking English but could understand and speak Yiddish, too.

In America, Jewish immigrants read Yiddish newspapers and saw Yiddish plays. Audiences laughed at comedies about immigrant life and cried at tragedies such as Shakespeare's *King Lear* performed in Yiddish translation.

In Rebecca's time, Americans also enjoyed *vaudeville* shows, which had a variety of song and dance acts, comedians, magicians, and even animal acts. New York's vaudeville theaters were very grand and could seat an audience of thousands. Many movie actors got their start in vaudeville, just as cousin Max did.

The New Amsterdam Theatre showed vaudeville and, later, movies.

The Marx Brothers were vaudeville comedians before becoming comedy movie stars.

A 1914 movie poster

Even more popular than stage shows were the new motion pictures. By 1914, vaudeville theaters were showing feature films, too. Movie serials were all the rage, and on weekends young people flocked to serials like *The Perils of Pauline*. Serial episodes often ended in a *cliffhanger*, or suspenseful event, such as the heroine about to be run over by a train. Audiences would have to wait two weeks for the next episode to find out whether she survived!

Although they enjoyed seeing plays and movies, most adults did not view acting as a respectable way to earn a living. Actors were poorly paid and often out of work. Most parents didn't want their children to become involved in show business. A stagestruck teenager might have to run away from home to join an acting troupe!

Still, disapproval of the actor's lifestyle didn't stop people from flocking to movie theaters, and when

The actress Pearl White, who played Pauline

the first World War broke out in Europe in July of 1914, people had yet another reason to go to the movies. Before the main feature, theaters often showed a *newsreel*, a short film that told about current events using photos, live footage, and reenactments. Newsreels about the war were exciting and informative.

Although America had not yet entered the war, immigrants were keenly interested in it, because the war involved the countries many of them had left. Jews were especially concerned about the safety of their relatives back in Russia, and they raised millions of dollars to help them.

By the fall of 1914, it was becoming much more difficult to *emigrate*, or move away, from Russia because of the war. Immigrant families like Rebecca's realized that if they were going to help their relatives come to safety in America, it was now or never.

Every Jewish family had a charity box, or pushke, *to collect money for Jews in need.*

GLOSSARY

Bar Mitzvah *(bar MITS-vah)*—In Hebrew, this translates as "son of the commandment." It refers to the **ceremony** honoring a boy's first reading of the Hebrew Bible before the congregation, and refers also to the boy himself.

bubbie *(BUH-bee)*—the Yiddish word for **grandmother**

hallah *(HAH-lah; often spelled "challah")*—a Hebrew word for **a rich white bread** made with eggs and usually braided

kopek *(KOH-pek)*—a small **Russian coin**, similar to a penny

mitzvah *(MITS-vah)*—the Hebrew word for "commandment." For Jews, it means **a good deed,** or the duty to perform acts of kindness.

nudge *(nooj; same vowel sound as in "wood")*—in Yiddish, **a pushy pest**

oy vey *(oy VAY)*—a Yiddish exclamation meaning **"oh dear!"**

pushke *(PUSH-kee)*—in Yiddish, a small **can or box** used to collect money for charity

Shabbos *(SHAH-bes)*—Yiddish for **Sabbath,** the day of rest

shah *(shah)*—the Yiddish way to say **"shush!"**

trousseau *(troo-SOH)*—the **household goods** that a bride brings to her marriage. Originally a French word.

tsar *(zar; often spelled "czar")*—the Russian word for **emperor**

A SNEAK PEEK AT

Rebecca

AND ANA

*At last, Ana has arrived, all the way from Russia!
Rebecca can't wait to show her cousin around New York,
but Ana doesn't seem very happy to be here.*

ebecca squinted through the gray fog that blanketed New York Harbor. She could barely see the outline of the brick buildings at Ellis Island. That was where immigrants came when they first arrived in New York. Papa was there now, meeting Uncle Jacob and his family.

Rebecca had worried about Ana ever since Uncle Jacob's telegram arrived a few weeks ago. *Escaped Russia with great difficulty. Arriving New York 8 November 1914.* Ana had been ill before she left Russia. Was her health the "great difficulty" Uncle Jacob had mentioned?

If only Ana survived the journey safely, Rebecca was sure they would become as close as sisters. As the wind began to scatter the thin gray wisps of fog, she saw a small ferryboat chugging across the harbor. Behind it, the Statue of Liberty stood out against the clouds.

"Do you think Ana's on that ferry?" she asked, turning to her family. "We've been waiting for hours."

Rebecca's grandparents huddled together

against the wind. Bubbie pulled her kerchief tighter around her head, and Grandpa pulled his scarf up around his neck. Rebecca's little brother, Benny, stood on a bench, watching the boats. Her older brother, Victor, held on to Benny's collar so he wouldn't tumble over.

"It takes a long time to get through Immigration," Mama said.

Grandpa shook his head, remembering. "So many people! Such lines! We shuffled into line to get off the ship. We stood in line to go into the building, *schlepping* everything we owned. Then another line while we walked up those steep stairs, praying nobody thought we looked sick."

"I should think *everyone* would feel sick after two weeks sailing across the ocean," said Rebecca's sister Sadie.

Sadie's twin, Sophie, looked sympathetically at her grandparents. "You must have been so anxious."

Bubbie nodded. "If inspectors thought something was wrong, they might not let us into America."

"When we were on the ship," Mama said, "other

passengers warned us about passing through
Immigration. Just because you land in New York,
it doesn't mean you can live here. The officials keep
out anyone who has a serious illness. If they think

you have a problem, they mark a letter on
your coat with chalk. An *E* means you
might have an eye disease. *H* means you
might have a heart problem. There's a
long list."

Rebecca had heard lots of stories about Ellis
Island from her friends at school. When immigrants
had a disease that could spread, officials sent them
back to the country they came from.

Rebecca remembered what her friend Rose
had told her about immigrants who were sick when
they arrived. "*Contagious disease*, they call it," Rose
said. "You got one, you go back. That's it. And the
ship company has to pay for your ticket." Rebecca
tried to forget about Rose's words. She could only
hope Ana was well enough to climb the stairs
at Ellis Island.

Mama's cousin Max paced along the walkway.
Now that he was an actor with a movie company, he
had helped pay for the tickets. "I've got an idea,"

Max said, flashing his sparkling smile. "Let's practice a little welcoming song to greet the family when they step off the ferry. We'll sing 'You're a Grand Old Flag.'" Max started singing softly.

Rebecca knew the chorus, and so did the twins. Her sisters linked their arms as they chimed in. "You're a grand old flag, you're a high-flying flag, and forever in peace may you wave . . ."

When Rebecca no longer knew the words, she hummed along. She listened carefully as Max sang. He made every word sound exciting! "You're the emblem of the land I love, the home of the *free* and the *brave* . . ." He emphasized some of the words, giving the song more rhythm. Bubbie nodded in time to the music, and Grandpa tapped his foot. Benny marched around them in a small circle, saluting every time he passed Max.

A loud horn blast whistled through the air, and Benny covered his ears. The ferry pulled up to the dock, smoke belching from its smokestack. Rebecca stretched up on her toes, trying to see the passengers on deck. Hundreds of people crowded at the railing in strange-looking clothing—rough black coats, long scarves that fell past their knees, odd flat caps and summer straw hats. Their arms were weighed down with featherbeds, quilts, and bulging carpetbags, yet their tired faces glowed with excitement.

"There's Papa!" Rebecca exclaimed. She jumped up and down, waving in his direction. Papa had gone to Ellis Island to sign papers proving that Uncle Jacob and his family had someone to help them settle in America. Rebecca searched the crowd anxiously, trying to guess which girl was her cousin. Even if Ana was sick, the immigration officials wouldn't send her back to Russia alone, would they?

"Start singing," Max directed them.

Above the din of shuffling feet and shouted greetings in many languages, Rebecca sang with all her might.

"Over here!" Mama called, and Rebecca saw Papa standing next to his brother. Rebecca thought she would have recognized Uncle Jacob anywhere. Although he looked older than Papa, with streaks of gray in his hair and beard, he looked very much like her father. Beside him, Aunt Fanya looked pale and weary. Her shoulders slumped, and her eyes were rimmed with dark circles. A boy a bit taller than

Victor waved his hand toward them. He must be either Michael or Josef.

Then Rebecca saw a girl about her own age, right behind Aunt Fanya. It had to be Ana, but she looked nothing like Rebecca had imagined. Her cheeks were smudged with streaks of dirt. Her face looked thin and drawn under her wool scarf, but the rest of her bulged, and her clothes pulled at their buttons. Like the other immigrants, she had a large passenger tag pinned to her coat, which flapped in the breeze.

Rebecca glanced at the crowd behind them. Where was Ana's other brother?

Read All of Rebecca's Stories,
available at bookstores and *americangirl.com.*

Meet Rebecca
When Rebecca finds a way to earn money,
she keeps it a secret from her family.

Rebecca and Ana
Rebecca is going to sing for the whole school.
Will cousin Ana ruin her big moment?

Candlelight for Rebecca
Rebecca's family is Jewish.
Is it wrong for Rebecca to make a
Christmas decoration in school?

Rebecca and the Movies
At the movie studio with cousin Max,
Rebecca finds herself in front of the camera!

Rebecca to the Rescue
A day at Coney Island brings more
excitement and thrills than Rebecca expected.

Changes for Rebecca
When Rebecca sees injustice around her, she
takes to the streets and speaks her mind.